Laura Sheldon is a teacher ~~~~~~~~~~ he Vale of Glamorgan where there is a real writers' shed overlooking the sea.

'I was born and brought up in Hillside Crescent in Swansea, around the corner from where Dylan was born. I've always enjoyed writing and creating stories. When I became a primary school teacher in 2000 I found lots of opportunities for exploring this with my pupils; everything's more fun taught through a story!'

Huw Aaron is a freelance cartoonist and illustrator living in Cardiff, whose drawings have appeared in places such as *Private Eye*, *Reader's Digest* and the Firefly book *Steve's Dreams: Steve and the Sabretooth Tiger* by Dan Anthony. He has a rugby comic strip, North Stand and a webcomic called *Blart*.

for Tom, Alice and Charlie
and all their adventures

Mr Manli's Shed

and a ghost named Dylan

by

Laura Sheldon

Firefly

First published in 2014
by Firefly Press
25 Gabalfa Road, Llandaff North, Cardiff, CF14 2JJ
www.fireflypress.co.uk

Text © Laura Sheldon 2014
Illustrations © Huw Aaron 2014

Laura Sheldon and Huw Aaron assert their moral rights to be identified as the
author and illustrator in accordance with the Copyright, Designs and Patent
Act, 1988.

A CIP catalogue record of this book is available from the British Library.

Print ISBN: 978-1-910080-17-7
Epub ISBN: 978-1-910080-16-0

This book has been published with the support of the Welsh Books
Council.

Typeset by: Elaine Sharples

Cover design by Liz@madappledesigns.co.uk
Dragonfly series design by Laura Fern Baker
Extract from 'Fernhill' with kind permission of the Dylan Thomas estate

Printed and bound by: Bell and Bain, Glasgow

Contents

One

Mr Mahli

Everybody likes Mr Mahli. Some old men can be grumpy and disagreeable; they scowl at noisy children and bark back at yappy dogs. Some old men are nice enough but no one really notices them. They shuffle along in flat caps and beige jackets as slowly as milk floats. I bet you know a few of these. Perhaps one or two even live on your

street. But I'd be very surprised if you know their names.

Mr Mahli is different. If you have a Mr Mahli on your street then you are one lucky person, because (as you may have heard people say before) everybody likes Mr Mahli.

Why? I hear you ask. Well, let me tell you. You know when you're walking down the street with your mum and you meet another grown-up that you know. They stop and say 'Hello' and they chat to your mum. They might look at you and say 'Hello there!' and you notice that they change their voice ever so slightly (usually make it just a bit higher) and they smile with their mouths and then go right back to talking to your mum? Well, Mr Mahli is the total opposite of this. When he meets children he knows, he doesn't just think 'small person alert: must smile, nod and ignore', he actually knows their names, what they love doing best, what they are totally mega-brilliant at and sometimes the things they may be a teensy bit rubbish at too. So he talks to the kids just like he talks to the adults, and some adults would be surprised at how this makes him stand out.

He also knows tricks, magic tricks. You can be walking past his house, minding your own business, when you might spot something very strange like a tiny bright-red rabbit hopping out of the gate. You tip-toe up to it, put out a cautious hand to stroke it and POUFF! It turns into a silky red handkerchief and Mr Mahli is leaning over his fence, chortling merrily at you.

Sometimes he makes you laugh when you least expect it. Take last March for instance. It was the St David's Day Eisteddfod down at the town hall and it was all getting a bit boring. Dafydd Holmes had the microphone and had just discovered how soothing yet exciting he found the sound of his own voice. Nine-year-old Tomos Brown was sitting next to his Nan Taylor (whom Mr Mahli always describes as a bit of a hottie) and Mr Mahli was sitting opposite them on a chair next to the stage. He was waiting to present the cup to the winner in the over-90s' category.

Tomos looked over at Mr Mahli who winked, then widened his brown eyes and nodded towards Tomos' Nan. Tomos gave her a nudge and pointed at Mr Mahli. As she turned her head to look at him, he stretched out one leg and flexed his foot at Nan Taylor. On the soul of his shoe he had written in black biro the words 'I love you'. Nan chuckled quietly, blushed and shook her head. Satisfied, Mr Mahli lowered his leg. But before Nan could turn back to the stage he had lifted his other leg, baring the sole of the other shoe, on which was written '…but not very much'. Tomos heard his Nan breathe in quickly and when he looked at her face he saw she was trying desperately not to laugh.

Two

The Shed

Anyway, that is just what Mr Mahli was like. Fun. He lives on Hillside Crescent and always has done since his parents moved to Swansea from India way back in Prehistoric Times. He told his young neighbour, Alys, that if he had been born in India he would have been a prince, but that gypsies had tried to capture his mother and she and his father had decided to flee the country and live in anonymity in South Wales.

His house is one of the neatest in the street. In the little front garden he has shaped the bushes into wild animals. He has a giant eagle, an African elephant and a cat (which was supposed to be a panther). But the back garden is the best. He grows rows of plump shiny vegetables and fruits that smell amazing and fill the pockets of the children who come to play. He has a massive climbing tree that you can climb up then swing down, off a huge bendy branch. Right next to the house is a really deep pond with super-friendly fish that come up to the surface when the children throw food at them, gaping and snapping their little fishy jaws.

The only slightly spooky thing about the garden is the shed. Not the tool shed where Mr Mahli keeps his lawn mower and banana boat and things like that, but the old shed behind it. That was the only place where Mr Mahli had forbidden the children to play. A couple of times they had dared each other to stand on someone's shoulders and peek in, but they always came down disappointed and confused. That was the weird thing you see. The shed had nothing in it. There weren't even any tools or old flowerpots or spiders or anything else that people keep in their garden sheds.

It was totally

completely

empty.

So why did Mr Mahli have an empty wooden shed in his garden? Well, he actually had many explanations for this. That's what was so confusing. Every time somebody asked Mr Mahli about the shed he gave them a different story to explain why it was there, why nobody was allowed in and why it was always empty.

Here are two of my personal favourites:

1. The Pirates' Shed

It actually belongs to the pirates who smuggled Mr Mahli's family out of India and he is honour-bound to keep it in his garden forever. Now and again the pirates bring treasure to hide in the shed, which is why no one must go in. The pirates are a ruthless bunch and they would happily slit the throat of anyone they found in their secret shed.

2. The Time Machine

It is not actually a shed but a highly sophisticated time machine, painted to look like a shed. It looks like there's nothing in it because Mr Mahli used magic paint on the window to paint an 'inside-a-shed' scene in case of nosey parkers. He painted it empty so thieves wouldn't break in. If anyone steps inside the shed without the proper training and health and safety instructions they would instantly find themselves in India in 1923, which is where

Mr Mahli's parents came from. He flits between these two time zones because they are his favourite and the best and he should know because he has travelled throughout the Whole of Time.

Believe it or not neither of these stories were true. Tomos Brown found out the real reason for the shed the day after Mr Mahli went on holiday. And the truth was just as strange as the tales.

Three

TB

Tomos Brown lives on Hillside Crescent, across the road from Mr Mahli. He is nine years old and lives with his mum and his dad. Everybody calls Tomos 'TB' for short. His mum had tried to stop them because she thought it sounded like a disease, but nobody took any notice and now even his mum can be heard calling him TB when she's not concentrating.

TB loves messing about outdoors and riding his bike (especially off-roading). He doesn't have any brothers or sisters but that doesn't matter because he lives next door to the best nine-year-old girl in the world. Her name is Alys James and TB thinks she is alright because she isn't really like a girl at all. She loves to climb trees and play football and go surfing with TB and his dad. She eats just as much

as TB and doesn't worry about getting her clothes messy. She is actually better than him at Temple Run but TB wouldn't admit that.

Alys and TB spend a great deal of weekend time in Mr Mahli's garden (especially since their mums agreed that iPads were strictly for Rainy Days). Last autumn he'd helped them to complete a truly epic joint project for school on 'Weather' by setting up some weather-recording instruments in his garden, all homemade from the most ordinary of household objects. Wire coat-hangers were fused with baked bean tins and TB's Lego cogs in an ingenious way. The project had impressed Mr Davies beyond measure and he'd awarded them tons of house points as well as a 'magical prize from the magical box of magical prizes' each.

Anyway, this story isn't about projects and prizes. But it does begin in Mr Mahli's garden, where a lot of interesting things begin.

Four

Mr Mahli's Holiday

One Saturday TB headed over to call for Alys but she'd already left to go shopping with her mum. As he turned to go back home TB noticed a taxi outside Mr Mahli's house, sitting there with its engine running. Out of curiosity and boredom TB wandered over to see where Mr Mahli was off to at that time

in the morning. He was bustling out of the door, his arms full of suitcases and a hat. A truly awful hat actually, but this isn't a fashion commentary either.

'Morning Mr Mahli!' TB called over the noise of the diesel engine.

'Ah! *Shwmae* young Tom,' he replied. 'Lovely day for it isn't it?'

'Lovely day for what? Where are you off?'

'Cardiff airport *bach*. Trip of a Lifetime.'

You could hear the capital letters as he spoke.

'Where's that to then?' TB shouted back as he ran to hold the gate open for Mr Mahli.

'India. The motherland. I've got a whole itinerary sorted, Taj Mahal, trip on The Ganges, the lot. I'll be gone for three weeks in all. Actually,' he continued as he lowered his suitcases into the open boot, 'glad I ran into you. Got a big favour to ask.'

TB nodded and stepped back from the car, his head still full of images of an exotic, glimmering India.

'I need you to water the veggie patch for me if you would. Keep an eye on the toms, they'll be ready soon and will need picking. Get that Alys to help you out, OK?'

'Course Mr Mahli, my dad loves your tomatoes.'

'Thanks boy.' Mr Mahli smiled and ruffled TB's hair, then he was off in the car and chuntering down the street. Off on his Holiday of a Lifetime.

And the garden belonged to TB.

He played in it for the rest of the morning, climbing and swinging down from the tree at least fifty times. He found a thick piece of rope wound around an old water butt and slung it over the jutting-out branch of the oak tree to make a swing which he dangled from for ages, until he decided it would be a lot more fun playing in the garden with Alys. TB checked his watch and was surprised to see that it was nearly lunchtime. He ran out of the garden towards his own house, noticing Alys' mum's car turning into the street as he reached his front door.

After lunch TB's dad announced that the conditions were perfect for nine-year-old learner surfers at Langland Bay. TB forgot all about Mr Mahli's garden as he helped his dad load the boards onto the car roof and pulled damp wetsuits down from their hangers in the garage.

It wasn't until TB was drifting off to sleep in bed that night that he remembered he was in charge of the best garden in the street. As he closed his eyes and let images of the garden run through his mind he suddenly thought about the shed. This was his chance! He had three weeks to explore. Three weeks to investigate. He didn't really believe any of the fairytales, but there was something not quite right, something fishier than the fishpond. And TB had every intention of finding out everything he could.

Five

Breaking in

The next morning TB amazed his mum by being dressed even before breakfast. He ate only two Weetabix (compared to his usual four), declined 'special treat toast' (toast in bed – a terrible idea which generated loads of crumbs but which his family had enjoyed since he was a baby) and headed out of the door, calling over his shoulder that he was off to look after Mr Mahli's garden.

Alys was also surprised to see TB up so early and standing on her doorstep. He hopped from one foot to the other as he explained about Mr Mahli's holiday and his plans to investigate the shed. Alys was slightly less interested it has to be said. You see, she had her own theory about the shed. She believed that it was simply an old shed that Mr

Mahli hadn't yet bothered to get rid of. Because everybody made such a fuss about how weird it was to have an old empty shed in an otherwise epic garden, he kept it as an excuse to invent mad stories. He loved nothing more than an audience Mr Mahli, and Alys knew that.

Eventually TB persuaded Alys that it actually was a great idea to get dressed and venture out into the chilly morning instead of snuggling up in her pjs and watching TV. The two friends were through the gate and standing in front of the shed in minutes.

'Well then. Are you going to try the door or what?' Alys prodded TB in the arm.

'Yeah! Course. But it's bound to be locked.'

'Don't know if you don't try it, do you?' Slowly she reached out an arm, but TB pushed her back.

'Hang on Al, let me go first.'

'Oy! Why should you? I reckon you're a bit scared actually, TB. I think you've been listening too hard to Mr M. What if there's pirates waiting to slit your throat eh? What if…'

'Shut it Al, I'm going in,' TB announced, and he pushed down hard on the shed handle. It was locked.

Alys chuckled quietly. She wandered away from the shed and spotted TB's swing from the day before.

'Hey! This is new! Check me out!' she called as she backed up a little slope and wound the rope around her wrists. TB wasn't looking though. He was turning over stones around the base of the shed

and lifting up plant pots, looking for the key. He didn't see Alys swing through the air screaming like Tarzan, but he heard her land as the rope slipped from her grip and she ploughed into the carefully piled crates that Mr Mahli kept his seedlings in.

'Gahhh! Ouch! Ooof!' cried Alys as she struggled to her feet, picking leaves out of her hair and a worm out of her ear. 'Good grief that hurt my bum!' she moaned, rubbing the mud into the seat of her jeans.

TB came running over, 'Oh Alys, look at the crates! You muppet, now we're going to have to stack all these again, AND re-pot those things.' He gestured to the seedlings, looking rather pathetic on the grass. 'Yes, I'm fine, don't worry TB, I'm sure there's nothing broken.' Alys looked down at her hands and the red welts that were appearing from the ropes. TB groaned. 'Come on, let's get started, then we can look for the key. I've had an idea. There's a bunch of keys by the back door. They look pretty ancient but one of them might be for the shed.'

'What, *inside* by the back door?' Alys asked.

'Yes. Oh yeah, good point, we'll need a house key…'

'How about,' Alys suggested, 'we break into *just* the shed, instead of the house and the shed. That'd be enough crime-ing for one day.'

TB smirked at his friend and laid the pot he was holding back down on the grass. 'OK. Let's look for a weak spot.'

They circled the shed like sharks around a sinking rowing boat. Alys noticed a loose screw on one of the planks of wood next to the door. She bent down to pull it and with a bit of easing and wobbling and some grunts, the screw was out. TB pulled at the wood. 'I don't think we can pull this any further without snapping it,' he said. But just as Alys bent to check, her foot pushed a stone an inch to the left and TB spotted a silver glint on the ground. The children reached for it at the same time and as they lifted it out of the soil they saw they'd struck gold. Well, not literally gold but as good as. You see, they'd found the key.

TB pushed it into the lock and felt it turn easily. The door swung open to reveal the empty shed and the two friends stepped inside.

Six

Dylan

The air was cold inside the shed. Alys and TB moved closer together as they felt shivers creep over their skin. There was nothing in there. Just as they'd seen from the outside, the shed was empty. Yet they felt as though there was *something*. In a strange way, something that could be felt but not seen was in the shed with them. The door creaked in the wind and Alys jumped. 'I don't like it in here TB, it's spooky.'

'I know,' TB replied, 'there's something well odd … why is it so cold?'

'Ooo yes, it is! And it smells weird … like … cigarettes.'

'Cigars,' said a deep voice and the children screamed, leapt out of the shed as fast as they could

and ran, leaving the shed door swinging in the breeze. They didn't stop until they were safely in Alys' bedroom, two sets of doors securely closed behind them.

They just sat for a while. Two sets of wide eyes and a load of shallow breath. Alys watched a tiny bead of sweat run down TB's cheek and felt her hands shaking beneath her quilt. Eventually the children felt themselves calm down, their breath slowing back down to a normal pace and that awful spiky feeling on their backs subsided.

'Alys...' TB started, 'we've got to go back.' He chewed on his bottom lip and waited for Alys' response. It came pretty quickly.

'Go back there? No way! Not if you paid me like a huge ton of money and ... and ... I dunno, like, gave me life-time free entry to Oakwood and ... and offered to do all my homework for the rest of my life! Like Forever! Not even then, Tomos Brown. There's something in that shed and I've never felt so scared in all my whole life!'

'Well, you *are* only just nine,' TB mumbled to Alys' feet. Before she could shout at him anymore,

TB got up and crossed the room. He turned to look at Alys as he pulled the door and sighed. 'Look Al, if we don't go back who'll shut the shed door? And we've left the garden in a right mess and all. Mr M trusted me! He asked me pacifically to look after his garden and now look!'

Alys smirked. 'It's *specifically*, you muppet,' she retorted.

'Please come,' Tom said, begging his friend with his eyes. 'I bet you still want to know *what* it is in there, don't you?'

Alys did want to know. She wanted to know really badly. But she was also worried that she would wee in her knickers if she saw or heard anything else remotely ghosty. Eventually she struck upon an idea. She hunted in the garage for a suitable form of defence. Something that would make her feel safer. Something that could possibly protect them both.

TB was very surprised to see his friend running out of her garage moments later, wielding a bicycle pump. She had a shaky grin on her face and waved the 'weapon' around proudly, point first, to show

TB. 'Riiiight,' said TB, 'what you going to do with that then?'

← Bike Pump!

'Look, it's just in case, alright? It's the only way I'm coming with you.'

They stood a little back from the shed this time. TB called out, 'Hello? Anyone in there?' and Alys giggled nervously. The children were both feeling jumpy and even the slight swinging of the door in the breeze had them twitching like bunny rabbits' noses. They inched forward, nudging each other, their breath sounding louder than ever before. TB swallowed the vast amount of saliva that seemed to have appeared in his mouth and reached out for the edge of the door. They both stood completely still as they heard the deep voice again, 'I don't bite you know. Haven't been able to for years.'

This time the voice sounded less scary, almost friendly and although the children jumped, they stayed rooted to the spot.

The air seemed to freeze around them. All the garden sounds were very far away at that moment, but the sound of the children's heartbeats thumped in their ears. They waited for an hour-long minute, then Alys waved her bicycle pump around half-heartedly by her feet.

'Is there someone here?' she whispered in a voice TB didn't recognise.

'There is…' replied the voice, 'but only if you know where to look.'

'Are you friendly or, like, crazy mental like…' started TB.

'Shh!' Alys shoved him gently. But to their surprise they heard a low chuckle.

'You look like the crazy ones with your – what is that – a bicycle pump? and your shaky legs,' laughed the voice. 'Come on in then, come and see for yourselves. I won't jump at you shouting "ooooo!" I promise you.' And the children felt themselves moving slowly, like ice cream slipping down a cone, into the shed.

Once inside, although they felt the coolness surround them, the children felt strangely calm and managed to remember how to breathe. But the shed still looked empty to them as their eyes adjusted to the dim light.

'Over here.' The voice was close but quieter, as though he didn't want to frighten them. 'You've got to look properly. Let your eyes relax and look into the corner by the window.'

The children followed the instructions, narrowing their eyes and frowning with concentration.

'What are you then?' Alys asked. 'You a ghost or something?'

'Exactly right I suppose,' replied the voice. 'Although I don't really think of myself as a ghost, I suppose I must be. Funny things us ghosts, you see. I feel like a man, like I did before … before it happened, but I'm not quite all there. I think I'm a little bit like an out-of-tune wireless; you can hear something through the crackling but it's not clear.'

'Like an out-of-tune what?' asked TB, but as he spoke he saw the shaky image of a man, sitting on a see-through chair, slowly come into focus.

TB gasped and backed up a little into Alys. 'What?' she demanded. 'What can you see?'

'Look over there,' TB pointed at the man, whose outline was rapidly filling in now. He could make out a mop of brown curly hair and a round nose above a cherubic mouth holding a cigar. The smoke peeling off the end of the cigar was also coming into focus; the smell suddenly hit TB and he coughed. 'Can't you see him Alys? You must be able to smell the…'

'Cigar?' Alys finished. As she sniffed the air she too started to see the smoke and followed the trail right down to the seated man.

'Who are you?' she asked, shaking her head in wonderment. 'And what are you doing in Mr Mahli's shed?'

The man smiled and said, 'My name's Dylan. And I've been in the shed for quite a few years now. It's kind of my home I suppose.' He looked surprised at this thought, as though he'd only just realised it and took another hard puff on his cigar.

'My question is...' he continued, 'what are you doing in here? And how come you can see me?'

Seven

A Very Strange Chat

Alys and TB looked at each other and shrugged. 'I've always wondered about this shed,' said TB. 'I've always wanted to know why it's here and why it's empty and Mr Mahli made up some amazing stories and well … I suppose I just wanted to know, y'know?'

Dylan nodded. 'Anyway, he's gone away on holiday, Mr Mahli, so I thought I'd come in, while he's away, just to see if … well, just to see. But how come we can see you? I don't know. You told us how to, didn't you?'

Both children could now see Dylan quite clearly. They could see the smoke too, curling round their bodies and settling on their hair. Alys stared at Dylan with a calm curiosity. 'Why are you here?

Were you a real person once? I mean before...' she asked.

'I was very real, me,' laughed the ghost, 'larger than life itself some said.' The children frowned at the small man. He didn't look very large or impressive. His tummy was quite round but he didn't look much taller than TB.

'I'm not sure why I'm here. It's hard to explain.' He sat back in his chair and closed his eyes as though sleeping, or thinking *really* hard. 'I've been

34

here a little while I think. But … not quite … whole. I have bits of memories coming to me now. It's very hard to see clearly. It's like if you have a dream, and when you wake up it's vivid in your mind, but then you try to tell someone about it and it's all … disjointed. You understand? Not … together.'

'Does Mr Mahli know you're here?' TB asked, moving closer to the figure to get a better look.

'Yes,' replied Dylan, defensively. 'He moved all the stuff out for me. He brings me these.' He gestured to his cigar. Alys glanced around the empty shed.

'But why did you want all the stuff out? Why do you want to sit all day in an empty shed?' she asked. Dylan smiled.

'Empty? You've got the wrong eyes on, *cariad*. It's not empty, look again.'

 This time, when Alys looked, she relaxed her gaze a little and sure enough shapes began to appear, like when your mum turns the light off

at night, but you're not tired, so you stare around your room in the dark and slowly you start to see things again.

There was a low bookcase, filled with shadowy books and mugs; a little stove in the corner with a glass door and a heavy black handle; a basket full of old papers and bits of wood and – pushed against the back wall – a wooden desk loaded with paper, pencils in a pot and frames with old pictures or photographs in, it was hard to tell.

'How did these things get here? This is seriously weird,' said TB, following Alys' gaze and noticing the objects for the first time.

'It is weird,' remarked Dylan. 'They weren't here at first. But gradually, as I started to think about and wish for things, they began to appear, just as I remembered them. I'm glad you can see them too. I thought I'd lost my mind for a while…'

The children eventually sat on the floor of the shed and talked to Dylan until their stomachs ached for food and they had to go home for lunch. They discovered that Mr Mahli had found Dylan in his shed years ago and had taken all the tools and plant pots out to make room for the ghost and his big imagination. He visited him sometimes and brought the cigars of course but otherwise left the ghost quite alone, for which he'd been grateful.

By the time the children left they had promised Dylan that they would be back the next day with something to eat. He hadn't tried before, but the cigars were so successful that he felt he'd like to give it a go.

Eight

Waitress Service

The next day was Monday and the children had to go to school. But as soon as they got home, they changed out of their uniforms and met by Mr Mahli's gate. TB had brought with him a Bounty bar and a packet of Munchies; thinking that if a person could manage to eat anything then it would be chocolate.

They still felt slightly anxious as they approached the shed. TB reached for Alys' hand, but her withering look made him snatch it back straight away. The strongest feeling they had though was excitement, they couldn't wait to see Dylan again and find out if he could eat real food. All day in school they'd been giving each other secret looks and little smiles, until Alys' friends had been convinced that TB was her new boyfriend! Of course Alys had been quite disgusted by this and made sure TB heard her telling them that wasn't the case At All.

They half-walked and half-ran round the back of Mr Mahli's garden towards the shed. Alys opened the door and together they entered the cool air of the inside. At first they couldn't see Dylan and their eyes desperately darted around as they searched for him. Then they heard a chuckle, which turned into a cough, and the image of a man began to shimmer into view.

'Hello there, that was quick,' said Dylan, rocking back in his chair. Alys frowned. 'Well, it's been a whole day and we're both keen to see if you can manage something to eat.' She turned to get the chocolate out of TB's hand and didn't notice the confused look on Dylan's face. 'Try it then,' she offered, holding out the chocolate. 'We didn't know what you'd like but, well, you can't *not* like Munchies, they're yum.'

Dylan reached out and tried to take the chocolate from Alys' hand but his fingers seemed to slip

through the bar and grasp at nothing. 'Mahli usually takes the packaging off my cigars, maybe that'd help,' he said.

TB took the Bounty and removed the wrapper but Dylan still couldn't hold it.

'We could try feeding it to you?' suggested TB but Dylan started to look a bit worried and Alys decided to change the subject.

'So, what have you been doing all day then?' she asked chirpily.

'Hmm, interesting question,' replied Dylan. 'You see, to me it seems as though you went out of that door just a couple of minutes ago. I suppose it's like I've been asleep but … I don't feel like I've just woken up.'

TB and Alys wondered about this for a minute, then TB said, 'I think maybe you're only a ghost some of the time. Perhaps the rest of the time you're where you should be … wherever all the other dead people are. But then you get bored and want to come back to almost alive again. Do you think? Is that what's happening to you?'

'I don't know. I didn't ask to be here, I'm not sure I even want to be here. I mean what's so great about being here if all I do is sit in a shed? Why choose that over eternal peace? Where's my choir of angels? Hey? Where's my white cloud?'

Dylan seemed to be getting himself quite worked up and TB and Alys felt themselves edging towards the door. But suddenly Dylan collapsed back in his chair with a sigh and rubbed his brow. The children just stood and waited. Eventually Dylan raised his head to look at them. 'Perhaps what I need, kids, is a change of scenery.'

Nine

A School Trip

Somehow Dylan managed to persuade TB and Alys to take him out of the shed. But not just for a walk. Not just to see the ducks in the park. Oh no, Dylan wanted more. He wanted to go to school.

Operation 'Moving Dylan' had to wait a few days as Alys and TB made arrangements and plans and tried to think of excuses. But on Thursday morning the pair left early to walk to school and slipped unnoticed into Mr Mahli's garden on the way.

Dylan had been practising making himself super-small because the plan was for him to fit inside TB's rucksack. As TB and Alys had needed to work hard to see Dylan in the first place, he was counting on the fact that their classmates would also find it difficult and as they weren't aware of Dylan's existence, hopefully they wouldn't even try to see him. Once he got to school he thought he'd be quite safe. Squeezing into the rucksack might be a trickier matter.

TB opened up his bag and took out the books and sandwich box, which he'd filled it with at home. Dylan put a tentative foot inside at first, then took a deep breath and jumped the other foot in and bent down. His bottom hung over the edge of the bag, his thick brown trousers straining against his bulk. TB and Alys tried very hard not to laugh and TB pulled the rucksack neck as wide as he could.

'It's no use Dylan,' said Alys, 'you're never fitting in there.'

'I'm big, I know that. But I'm not solid. I'm just a suggestion of a man, an outline with some misty innards. Squash me in mun, put your effort into it and *want* to do it. Use your will.'

Alys looked at TB and rolled her eyes. But the children lent forward and started to push Dylan as hard as they could into the bag. It was very weird at first. He felt like dry ice but sort of squashy. Sometimes TB's hand went right through him, but then he concentrated really hard and thought about what Dylan had said and suddenly, POP! Dylan was in the bag.

TB pulled the drawstring tight before Dylan began to expand again and the three friends set off down the garden path to go to school, excitement bubbling in their tummies (and in Dylan's misty, squashy dry ice).

They were a little late for school. The bell had already sounded and the last parents were just leaving as they slipped in through the gates. TB and Alys joined the end of their line and filed in after the other children. Mrs Best stood at the door of the cloakroom talking to Jamie Parkin (who had a lot to tell her about his hamster's cough and how it had kept him up all night) and TB managed to sneak past her with his bag. As the other children were putting things in their trays and getting out their books and having a chat, TB crept – ninja-style – into the teacher's cupboard at the back of the room.

He closed the door. The cupboard was dark with only a tiny high window letting in light through the dirt. It was cluttered too, with books, boxes, files and randomly a pair of wellies on the floor, but TB opened up the bag to show Dylan his temporary home anyway.

Dylan was not impressed.

'Now I remember why Mr Mahli was such a good host.' Dylan grumbled. 'You'll have to move some of this stuff out boy, there's no room for my things.'

'No way Dylan!' retorted TB. 'This is Mrs Best's cupboard. She can't even know I've been in here or I'll get in massive trouble. Look, it's not for long, just … just stay put and … shhh!'

'OK children, who's got their books out?' TB heard Mrs Best's voice very close to the cupboard. 'Well done, house point for you, Elen. And a house point for Jack. That's it Gregory, open your reading book.' She paused as the hubbub in the room died down. Pretty soon it was quiet. And TB was still in the cupboard.

Alys watched the cupboard door. 'Come on TB,' she muttered, 'what you doing in there?' Then she saw the handle begin to turn very slowly and deliberately and she realised Mrs Best was bound to notice. Unless …

'Mrs Best!' shouted Alys, getting to her feet. Mrs Best looked up from her register sharply. 'I've just remembered my mum really needed to see you!'

'Alright Alys, calm down! You gave me such a shock. I thought you'd spotted Gary Barlow in the playground.' (Mrs Best loved Gary Barlow more than chips.)

Alys sped across the classroom and opened the
door. Mrs Best got to her feet with a sigh and
followed Alys out of the room. TB saw his chance
and darted out of the cupboard and into his seat.
Seconds later Alys and Mrs Best marched back into
the room. 'I don't understand it, Mrs Best. She said
I was to get you and she'd wait in the yard.' Alys said,
acting all confused.

'Never mind, lovely,' replied Mrs Best, 'I'll give her a ring at playtime.'

Alys looked worried for a minute but then remembered her mum was working in the docks today and wouldn't be able to answer her phone. She hoped Mrs Best would forget all about it by the end of the day.

10

A Tiger Onesie

The day passed as uneventfully as a Thursday in Swansea usually does. Although TB and Alys kept glancing towards the cupboard, they never saw so much as a ghostly eye peeking through the slightly open door. Dylan was either behaving incredibly well … or he'd disappeared.

This thought occurred to TB just as the class was heading out for their afternoon play. He hung back from the line of children filing out of the door and sneaked over to the cupboard. 'Dylan,' he hissed 'you still in there?'

'Course I am boy,' came the reply 'just about made it comfortable. Did you happen to bring along any cigars?'

'No! I'm nine!' exclaimed TB. 'Where on earth would I get cigars? Anyway Dylan, you really shouldn't smoke you know.'

'Why the devil not boy?' Dylan looked down at his not-body, then back up at TB with a twinkle in his eye. 'It's not going to kill me is it?'

TB snorted. 'S'pose not. Anyway, what were you on about – you've made it comfortable? What've you been doing to Mrs Best's cupboard?' TB glanced around the shelves and floor, but he couldn't see anything out of place.

Dylan looked smug. 'Creative thinking, lad. Creative thinking.' His eyes stretched up to the ceiling and TB followed their gaze with his own.

There, up on the ceiling of Mrs Best's cluttered cupboard, was a perfect replica of the inside of Mr Mahli's shed. Dylan had projected his wishes around the single hanging light bulb and created his own upside-down den.

'How do you get up there?' TB asked in astonishment.

'I think it. Then I do it. You're not a free thinker boy, that's your problem. The only limits are the limits you give yourself,' Dylan declared grandly.

And with that, he took a deep breath, relaxed his legs and glided – almost gracefully – up to his comfy chair on the ceiling.

The effect was spoilt, ever so slightly, by the light bulb popping as Dylan's head drifted through it, and the cupboard plunging into darkness. But TB was suitably impressed and decided to leave Dylan there to go out to play, as he was quite safe and TB really needed a wee.

When the class came back they finished off their science and cleared away their things and it was time for them to go home. Mrs Best called out to the children, 'Right, the tidiest, most splendid, shiniest, smartest, most wondrous, fabulous…' the class frantically started tidying, they knew where she was going with this, 'cleanest table is going home first.'

During the frenzied rush to be the tidiest, most splendid, most shiny (oh, you get the idea) table, TB spotted Dylan's face peering over the top of the cupboard door. He looked around quickly, but no one else had noticed a thing. TB leant down to the rucksack under his desk and slowly pulled the drawstring open. When he looked up at Dylan however, Dylan was shaking his head. TB was confused, didn't Dylan *want* to go in the bag? He couldn't possibly want to stay in school *all night*. Urgh! Imagine that: a night in a dark, creepy, huge empty building. With spiders and rats and maths textbooks. TB shrugged his shoulders at Dylan and held the bag up towards him, but Dylan shook his head and pointed to the ceiling of the cupboard.

TB couldn't let it go. 'You're staying here all night?' he hissed incredulously. He was a little bit too loud and Mrs Best looked up sharply from her desk.

'No Tomos, I'm not staying here all night.' The children had mostly finished tidying and they stood behind their chairs, mildly listening to the conversation. 'Us teachers have homes to go to too you know.' She smiled.

TB nodded and began to explain that he knew that and that he wasn't talking to Mrs Best but then he stopped. If he wasn't talking to her, who was he talking to? That'd be a tricky one to explain. Anyway, it didn't matter because Mrs Best was on a roll now.

'We like to go home at the end of the day and put the telly on,' she continued. 'We make ourselves some yummy tea and take off our teacher masks.' Some children tittered. 'We like to snuggle down on our warm red sofas with a large mug of tea and a book. Even us boring old teachers enjoy getting cosy in our super-soft tiger onesies.' Mrs Best's hand flew up to her mouth and the class burst into giggles.

'Oh no!' Mrs Best cried, 'I've said far too much! What would happen to my reputation as a Very Serious Person if they all knew about the tiger onesie?' The class laughed again, the idea of their smart teacher in a tiger onesie was just ridiculous.

'Right,' Mrs Best began, in a stern voice, 'Year 4, stand up straight.' The children did as they were told (except Danny Gerard who'd found something far more interesting up his left nostril which needed all his concentration).

'Put one hand on your hearts. And one hand on your dictionary.' Hands shot out across the room. 'Repeat after me,' Mrs Best instructed, 'I do solemnly swear…'

'I do solemnly swear…' chorused Year 4.

'That I – insert your own name here…'

'That I Alys, Jac, Tomos, Casey…' Names were shouted out all over the classroom.

'Will never, ever, not ever tell anyone…'

'Will never, ever, not ever tell anyone…'

'About Mrs Best…'

'About Mrs Best…'

'Wearing a tiger onesie at home…'

'Wearing a tiger onesie at home…'

'With fluffy ears…'

'With fluffy ears…' giggled the class.

'And … a tail.'

The class erupted into laughter. A deep chuckle was amongst them but only Alys and TB heard it.

Seconds later everyone was pouring out into the yard. Another day at school done and a ghost left quite alone in the teacher's cupboard.

Eleven

Toilet Monitors

It was worrying TB and Alys that they couldn't speak to Dylan whenever they wanted to. He had been in the cupboard for nearly a week now, and although he hadn't caused any massive problems (Mrs Best always came out shivering and a couple of weird noises had caught some people's attention, but that was it) the children were not entirely happy with him being there.

The two friends sat on the wall in the yard one lunchtime and mulled the problem over. 'I tried to get in the classroom this morning, just before school, but Mrs Best always locks the door when she's not in there. I don't really fancy doing another Bond-style break in,' Alys said. 'Look what happened last time.'

TB looked thoughtful and rubbed his chin with his finger. Alys laughed, 'Alright Sherlock, you don't have to act like you're planning a major heist.'

'No, I'm not!' protested TB, 'I'm just getting the ketchup off.' And to prove it he stuck a slightly orange finger into his mouth. Alys wrinkled her nose and looked the other way.

'What we need,' said TB slowly, 'what we need, is a job.'

'What like fruit-tuck monitor?' asked Alys.

'Yes, exactly, but a job that means we can be in the classroom when no one else is around.'

'Good plan. What job?'

'I haven't got that far yet,' admitted TB. The pair sat in silence, trying to think of a job that would get them in the cupboard. Luckily, they didn't have to wait very long.

As the class sat painting with watercolours that afternoon, Gemma Bradley's hand shot up. 'Mrs

Best, please can I go to the toilet?' she jigged about a bit on her chair. Mrs Best sighed.

'Gemma, why didn't you go at lunchtime? You know you're not supposed to go in lesson time.' Teachers always tell you this but never believe that you genuinely didn't *need* to go at lunchtime. Gemma tried explaining but Mrs Best cut her off.

'Also Gemma, remember that if you need to go you have to ask in Welsh!'

Gemma was jigging a bit harder now and biting her lip with worry. Mrs Best noticed this and gestured towards the door.

'Go on then, Gemma,' she said, as Gemma dashed across the room. The rest of the class could hear her yell out as she ran towards the toilet, '*Ga i fynd i'r tŷ bach os gwelwch yn dda!*'

Mrs Best laughed and shut the door behind Gemma. Things carried on calmly for about ten minutes until suddenly Alys looked up and realised Gemma hadn't come back. She pointed this out to Mrs Best who sent Gemma's best friend, Eleni, out to see if Gemma was OK.

Eleni came back on her own. 'Mrs Best, there's no loo roll! Gemma's well upset, she says she's been sitting there for ages but she can't get up 'cos she needs to wipe and she's got no...'

'Toilet paper, yes I understand, Eleni. Hang on, I'll get some out of the cu...'

'I'll get it, Mrs Best!' called Alys, as she flew across the room and barged through the cupboard door. She presented the fresh roll of toilet paper to Eleni, who took it straight to her poor, stranded friend.

Alys saw her moment. Much to Mrs Best's surprise Alys and then TB proudly volunteered to become Singleton School's First-Ever Toilet Monitors.

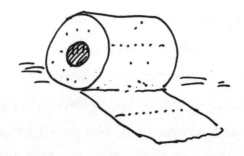

Twelve

A Little Close For Comfort

Playtime was the best time of day to collect fresh toilet supplies from the cupboard. Mrs Best *always* went to the staffroom for 'medicinal purposes' (coffee) and Alys was given the classroom key. On their first day in the job, Alys and TB ducked into the classroom and shut the door firmly behind them.

'Dylan? It's OK it's us,' stage-whispered TB, opening the cupboard.

'Oh the bog monsters is it?' came back the deep voice. 'Feeling a little *flush* are we? Just a *wee* bit smelly aren't you? Look at the state urine!' Dylan laughed heartily at himself. The children just sighed.

'None of that makes any sense, Dylan. You're hysterical,' commented Alys, 'and not like *ha ha*.'

'Look Dylan, it's only a matter of time before you blow your cover,' said TB. 'I think we've got to make a plan to get you out of here.'

Dylan stopped chuckling straight away and folded his arms tightly across his chest. 'I'm not ready to go,' he announced, 'I like it here and I've not been any trouble. I'm actually starting to feel a little bit more ... substantial in this cluttered cupboard. I may want to stay.'

'But you can't stay!' cried Alys. 'You can't possibly stay in school forever. What about Mrs Best? What about the summer holidays?'

'And what about Mr Mahli?' finished TB.

The children stared at Dylan, waiting for his response. They fully expected an argument. But Dylan lowered his arms (or raised them as he was upside-down in his chair on the ceiling) and suddenly looked sad.

'Mr Mahli,' he repeated. 'Yes, I suppose I'd almost forgotten about him. He's been a good friend to me that man. A good host. A man with no questions you know? A comrade.' Dylan nodded to himself as he thought about what he should do. After a couple of seconds he brightened. 'Well, we've got a week left haven't we? If the date on that board is correct, Mahli won't be back 'til then. So, we may as well keep me here for now. You two can come and check on me when you collect your … supplies, and I'll stay quiet as a spider the rest of the time.'

Alys and TB had to agree with this. One more week seemed perfectly reasonable. And if either of them were faintly suspicious of Dylan's promise, they didn't share it with the other and the pair left the cupboard and the classroom and went out to play, feeling ever-so-slightly uneasy for the rest of the day.

It was during English the next day that things started to go wrong. Mrs Best was out for the morning doing some sort of training and a supply teacher called Miss Terry was teaching instead. Danny Gerard had found this very amusing and tried calling out, 'It's a Miss Terry!' as the answer to every question but Miss Terry was more stern than mysterious and had quickly threatened him with a trip to the head teacher if he 'continued with that nonsense'.

Miss Terry had written the date and the focus for the lesson on the board and Dylan was interested to see the word 'Poetry' written in her neat, curling script. It was something he knew quite a bit about and his not-heart quickened a little as he thought of the possible ideas Miss Terry might give the children. Perhaps a bit of drama, a picture or an interesting object might be put before the class. Perhaps she'd read them some poems or play them some music.

'What are adjectives?' began Miss Terry. Polly Peter knew. She always knew stuff like that.

'Describing words, Miss,' she announced.

'Correct,' affirmed Miss Terry. 'Because you are looking at our solar system in your topic work, I'd like you to write a poem, using adjectives, to describe a planet. You write the name of the planet in capital letters down the side of your page, like this.' She demonstrated writing the word SATURN vertically down the page. 'Then you have to think of a word beginning with each letter, to start a sentence to describe the planet. Off you go now please. And do it without a sound.'

After this, she sat down, pulled a pile of maths books towards her and began to mark them swiftly, with harsh red pen.

Polly had already started, as had Amelia and David. But the rest of the class looked a little stumped. Alys leant over to TB and whispered, 'How am I supposed to describe a planet when I have no idea what it looks like or anything?'

'I know,' replied TB. 'I haven't got a clue. And look at Katie!' The children glanced over to where Katie was sitting to see a big fat tear land 'plop!' on her book. Katie couldn't do stuff like this on her own, Mrs Best always helped to start her off.

Dylan watched from the cupboard. He shook his head at the stern teacher, who seemed unaware of the crying child, and at the sight of the silent classroom where the children struggled to think of anything to write. The more he watched, the angrier he became. He stared at the word 'Poetry' boldly written on the board, giving a bad name to his favourite thing. He heard the boy nearest to the cupboard mutter to his friend, 'I hate poetry.' And that was that. Dylan squeezed his body out of the crack in the door and walked to the front of the class.

TB and Alys looked up in shock. 'No, don't!' cried TB before he could stop himself and Alys leaped to her feet. Miss Terry jumped up in surprise too, but her surprise was at the children, she didn't see the man standing by her side.

'What on earth are you two doing?' Miss Terry demanded. It took TB a couple of seconds (wide-open mouthed ones) before he could answer. Desperately looking around the class, he saw that all the other children were looking at him not at Dylan. His eyes stopped darting about and landed on Katie.

'It's Katie, Miss Terry. We were worried about her and thought she might be sick.'

Miss Terry frowned and turned to face Katie who (luckily for TB and Alys) was still sniffling and dropping tears on her book. 'Are you going to be sick, Katie?' Miss Terry asked with a grimace on her face. Katie saw a way out and nodded. 'Well then, take yourself off to the toilet, girl. Goodness me, we don't want a classroom full of sick people do we?' snapped the teacher. And poor Katie pushed her chair back and legged it.

Dylan stood very close to Miss Terry as she stood before the class. 'Everyone else get back to work,' she ordered, 'and no more rude disruption from you two.' She pointed the pen she was holding directly at TB and Alys and scowled at them. They sat down slowly, watching Miss Terry and Dylan all the time. Dylan cleared his throat loudly. Alys and TB gasped quietly at the sound of Dylan's cough and a few children looked up sharply. Miss Terry shivered suddenly and turned towards the open door. As she got up to close it, Dylan seemed to muster all his

strength and swung his arm round like he was bowling in a cricket match. To Alys and TB's surprise the pen shot straight out of Miss Terry's hand with such force that it hit the ceiling before falling to the ground.

'What … what.' Miss Terry looked at her hand, then at the pen on the floor, then back to her hand several times. 'Who did that?' she demanded, and narrowed her eyes at the children closest to her. Dylan smirked and moved closer to her again. He took a deep breath and blew, as hard as he could, on the back of her neck. Miss Terry's dark hair flew forward over her face and she screamed sharply as she ducked behind the desk. The children were confused and surprised but they couldn't help laughing at the sight of Miss Terry cowering behind her chair.

'Stop it at once!' she shrieked. 'Whoever is doing that, just stop it at once!' This wasn't the best thing to say to Dylan, who was really enjoying Miss Terry's reaction. With an elaborate sweep of his arms he pushed the books and papers off Mrs

Best's desk. Miss Terry screamed again and the children jumped out of their chairs to get a better look. They watched in amazement as Miss Terry flapped around amongst the books, trying to get to her feet. The ones who were looking also saw a whiteboard pen lift up from the desk all by itself and hover over to the board. They were too surprised to call out to the rest of the class and just watched with open mouths and held breath as the pen put a wobbly line straight through the word 'Poetry' on the board.

Alys watched Dylan run to the other end of the classroom, holding his side and laughing like a moped engine. Suddenly he stopped and his face lit up. I don't mean like your face lights up on Christmas morning when you see your stocking, but really and truly lit up, as though a hundred tiny LED lights had been turned on underneath his skin. Alys pulled TB towards her.

'Look!' she urged 'look at him!'

TB pulled his gaze away from Miss Terry. The rest of the class were transfixed by her and were torn between helping, laughing or running to the toilet because the laughing had got too much.

'Woah!' exclaimed TB, 'what's he doing?' Dylan's glowing expression had turned quite serious. He seemed to be concentrating really hard on something. His body was crouching slightly and his hands were bunched into white fists. 'Oh no. What if it was all too much?' TB hissed in Alys' ear. 'What if something's happening to him? Should we go over?'

'No! Just stay put TB. He doesn't look upset or anything. He just looks as though he's … I dunno … trying to do something.'

'Uh, oh.' TB said quietly.

Miss Terry had finally managed to stand up and was ordering some of the children closest to her to pick up her books and pens. Her dark hair flew around her face wildly and her glasses sat at a jaunty angle on her hooked nose. She straightened her clothes and looked around for her left shoe. She was about to send someone to fetch the head teacher when there was a shout from the back of the classroom where Aled Phillips was sitting.

'Hey!' he called, 'check this out!' He held up a small piece of white paper. 'It just landed on my head! It says "kel … cel … celestial serenity". Molly! You've got one too!' Molly reached up to the crown of her head and picked up the paper she found there.

'Mine says, "Spiralling in the deep and silent darkness"!' she exclaimed. The children looked up at the ceiling and were amazed to see – with the slow-motion mistiness of a dream – little pieces of paper floating down like snowflakes all around them.

Soon the classroom was full of shouts of delight as the children read their paper flakes aloud and ran through them, holding out their arms and kicking the ones that had made it to the floor. Miss Terry took off her glasses and stared. Dylan had stopped glowing and sat with his arms on his bent knees, smiling like a child at the scene before him.

'Where did they come from?' people were shouting.

'What's happening?'

'Is it magic?'

'Magic,' repeated TB 'yes, it's certainly that.'

Miss Terry closed her mouth (it was feeling a little dry as she'd been holding it open for some time now) and started to clap her hands and call to the children to sit down and calm down. But the noise was too great and the children didn't really hear her. Suddenly Molly ran over to the board and stuck her paper as high up as she could reach.

'It's a poem!' she shouted 'look, I've started it. They're little pieces of poem. I think we have to put them together.'

The children started to move back towards their seats, their little bits of paper gathered in their hands like pirate treasure. Joseph was next to get the idea. He stuck his paper next to Molly's. 'Listen to this,' he called and grandly read the beginning of the poem to the class. 'Who's next?' he asked. 'Miss Terry, this is brilliant.'

Miss Terry stood up and began to speak but she was drowned out by Alys who ran to the board with a piece of paper she'd found on her shoulder.

'Floating sphere of perfect symmetry,' she blurted as she added the paper to the poem.

'Woo-hoo!' called TB and clapped his approval loudly.

'Miss Terry,' said TB, 'this is the best poem lesson ever. Clap for Miss Terry everyone!'

The class joined him in a muted round of applause. Miss Terry had never had a clap before. She'd never had anyone say her lesson was 'the

74

best' before. She pursed her lips and nodded tightly.

The class continued to build the poem. They kept reading it and adding to it and moving it about until the bell went for lunchtime. Miss Terry watched them go, then ran, out of the classroom, out of the school and all the way home to cwtch her old teddy under the bed covers for at least twelve hours.

Thirteen

When You Gotta Go...

Alys and TB hadn't enjoyed the fall-out from Dylan's little tricks. The whole class had to stay in at playtime when Miss Terry failed to turn up the next day and rang the school to complain that her nerves weren't up to it, and the head teacher had been called to give them a proper telling-off. Nobody could quite

explain what had happened and this seemed to make the grown-ups even more cross. A couple of children had tried to tell Mrs Best about the floating pen and the books that moved by themselves but she had shaken her head and looked disappointed so they quickly stopped trying to tell her the truth.

'Right, Dylan. That's it. You've gotta go.' TB had sneaked back at the end of school while Mrs Best was chatting to a parent.

'Look, I know it wasn't clever but I couldn't just watch that old goat carry on like that,' protested Dylan, 'and you all had a good laugh didn't you?'

'No, I didn't! I was too busy wondering what they'd do with you if they saw you,' cried TB. 'I thought they'd call in the vicar and do an exercise on you or something!' Dylan frowned briefly then got it.

'Exorcism you mean.'

'Oh whatever, Dylan. The point is, you promised you'd be good and quiet and not get us into trouble and it's all going pear-shaped. You have to go, Dylan. The school trip is over.'

Dylan smiled at TB's worried face and nodded gently. 'All right boy, all right, I'll go. You're right and I'm wrong. Although you're nine and I'm … God knows how old, I'll defer to your inner wisdom and do as I'm told.'

'Does that mean you'll leave?' TB just wanted to check, he found Dylan confusing sometimes.

'I'll go. I'll leave this place tomorrow upon my word. I just need one more day here. I've got one more thing I want to try,' Dylan stated.

'What? What do you want to try? It's not going to cause…'

'Don't worry, boy,' Dylan whispered. 'No one will know I'm here, I promise.'

TB realised that Dylan was whispering because Mrs Best had come back into the classroom. He grabbed a couple of toilet rolls from the shelves, nodded briefly at Dylan and backed out of the door.

There wasn't a peep from Dylan the following day. Mrs Best had even played, 'Who's in the cupboard?' with the class (*a great but pretty pointless game in which someone goes out of the room whilst someone else hides in the cupboard and the first person has ten seconds to guess who's hiding. It's surprisingly exciting actually)* and nobody had noticed anything weird about the cupboard.

Alys had asked Mrs Best to help her find her lost jumper at the end of the day to give TB a clear go at fetching Dylan. TB waited until the classroom was empty then opened his backpack as wide as he could and called out to Dylan. There was no reply.

TB dashed over to the cupboard and pushed open the door. His gaze was met with a Dylan-free space. There was no trace of his round body or his bookcase or the faint chill in the air. He was completely gone.

Fourteen

Mr Mahli's Return

It seemed as though the rest of the week whizzed by like a few days of birthdays. Although Alys and TB had searched the whole school, they hadn't managed to find Dylan or any sign that he'd ever been there. Alys started to wonder if she'd dreamed the whole thing. It was only TB's determined face that kept her looking.

They'd been so busy, they'd almost forgotten about toilet duty and had been sternly told off by Danny Gerard after he'd been caught short Friday lunchtime. Alys had been to see Mrs Best about giving up toilet monitoring but Mrs Best had said that they ought to give it a proper try and they were setting a very good example and something about 'work ethic' that they hadn't understood. In the end

Alys had to agree that they'd keep it up at least until the end of term.

It was whilst TB and Alys were collecting supplies from the cupboard that they decided they had to tell Mr Mahli that they'd lost Dylan when he came back the next day. 'He might have an idea about where he's gone,' said Alys.

'Yeah, maybe he's done this kind of thing before,' agreed TB. The children sighed and finished their jobs worrying about what Mr Mahli was going to say.

It was windy and grey when TB knocked on Alys' door the following morning. She came plodding down the stairs in her pyjamas when her mum called her; hair sticking up at the back like an abandoned birds' nest. 'I'm not feeling well TB, think I'll just go back to bed. Come over later if you like, once you've, you know, talked to Mr M and that.'

TB shook his head.

'Oh no you don't Al, you're not leaving me to do this on my own. We both broke in, we both lost

Dylan, we both have to tell Mr Mahli.' TB seemed very definite about this and Alys found herself reluctantly reversing her steps.

She was, as I've said before, the best nine-year-old girl ever after all, and she wasn't really about to leave her friend to take all the blame. She came downstairs a minute later, wearing jeans and a Wales rugby top, a beanie pulled down over her birds' nest hair and a smudge of toothpaste on her chin.

'Let's do it,' she declared.

Mr Mahli was overjoyed to see them; the garden was in excellent shape and he praised TB and Alys for their professional-style care of the tomatoes. He'd enjoyed the swing TB had made too, and proudly showed them his mud-stained jacket which he'd gained from doing an 'epic jump off the top'. The children wandered out into the garden with him and listened to his chatter and almost began to consider not telling him after all. Perhaps he wouldn't notice Dylan had gone, or more likely, he'd think that he'd simply disappeared in a spooky, ghostly Dylany way.

But whilst Mr Mahli was filling them in on India and the magical sights and sounds he'd seen, the children knew they had to be honest. He deserved to know the truth.

'Mr M,' began TB, 'we've got something to tell you.' Mr Mahli stopped talking and walking and turned towards TB. He recognised the seriousness in TB's voice.

'OK,' he said, 'shall we sit down on the bench?' He led the children over to the most sheltered part of the garden where they cwtched up close on the wooden bench, out of the wind.

TB didn't quite know what to say, so he shuffled his feet around a bit and stared at the floor until Alys decided to take control.

'We met Dylan,' she announced. Mr Mahli raised his eyebrows but didn't say anything. Alys thought she should go on. 'We went into the shed and met Dylan. So we know all about him and … we…'

'So you *broke into* my private shed?' asked Mr Mahli. The children nodded. 'The place I'd asked you never to go into; I *trusted* you not to go into.' He let these words sink in for a minute before he continued. 'There are some things you just can't help yourselves to you know, you have to respect other people and their property and their privacy.' The children nodded again. Alys looked as though she might cry.

'We haven't told anybody though Mr M. We haven't said anything, I promise.' TB looked earnestly into Mr Mahli's warm brown eyes and was surprised to see them crinkle up in a smile.

'Alright then, tell me all about it. You been keeping him company for me? I hope he hasn't got you to buy him cigars!' Alys laughed and launched into the story of how they'd managed to find the key and open the shed (although in this version she made herself sound a lot braver than she had actually been, TB thought).

'But the thing is Mr Mahli…' TB chipped in. 'He was a bit restless in your shed. He really wanted a change of scene. He said he was … bored.'

'What do you mean?' asked Mr Mahli. 'He's been happy in that shed for years. Certainly never mentioned any scene-changing!'

'Well he did to us,' said Alys, 'and he somehow got us to take him on a trip.'

'A trip?' exclaimed Mr Mahli 'Where? What kind of trip?'

'We … took him to school,' admitted TB.

Mr Mahli fell off the bench.

As the children helped him up by hooking their hands into his armpits, he bombarded them with questions. The children had no time to reply though, before Mr Mahli set off like a train of determination towards the shed.

'Hang on!' TB called after him. 'He's not there!'
Mr Mahli turned suddenly.

'Not there? You haven't gone and left him in school have you?'

'Yes,' squeaked Alys, 'or we thought we had, but, well, he's not there now either.'

The children braced themselves for the explosion, but it never came. Instead Mr Mahli walked towards them very slowly and spoke very quietly (which was ten times more scary to be honest). 'If he's not there either, then where is he?' TB did an audible cartoon gulp then whispered, 'We lost him.'

'You what?' asked Mr Mahli quickly.

'We … lost him,' repeated TB.

'He tricked us!' Alys insisted. 'He said he'd come home with us yesterday if we'd just let him stay for one more day. But we went to the cupboard to fetch him and there he was, gone! We've looked all over the school and everywhere between it and your shed and we still can't find him.'

'We think he might have just … disappeared,' added TB. 'You know, gone back to ghost land or wherever he came from.'

The children waited for Mr Mahli to agree, to tell them that it was all going to be OK and that it wasn't their fault. But he stayed silent for several minutes (which is a really long time when you're waiting to find out if you're in trouble or not). Finally he spoke. 'We have to find him. He can't have gone too far. How the devil did you get him out of the shed anyway?'

'He got in my backpack,' said TB. Mr Mahli looked at the bag.

'How did he get in there? He's not a slight man.'

'No,' confirmed TB, 'but he managed to sort of squish himself up. He settled nicely in Mrs Best's

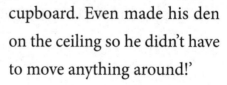 cupboard. Even made his den on the ceiling so he didn't have to move anything around!'

Mr Mahli didn't look as impressed as TB thought he might have been. He chewed his bottom lip for a minute

then breathed in deeply and pushed himself up off the bench.

'Right. I'll go and search for him. I have ninja blood in me you know, I will be stealth-like and sneaky and I'll find that Dylan, you mark my words.'

TB and Alys nodded, impressed.

'Cool. I'll come too,' volunteered Alys. 'I've got an epic ninja costume, all black with a balaclava! I'll just go and…'

'No no, Miss James,' insisted Mr Mahli, 'you go home. It's starting to rain a bit so your mum might let you build that new Minecraft world. I'll be fine and I'll let you know if I find him.'

If he had a cape Mr Mahli would have swung it dramatically. But he didn't so he walked out of the garden sensibly, shutting the gate behind him.

Fifteen

Whatever's Happened to Mrs Best?

Monday morning saw a tired TB call for Alys to walk to school. They knocked on Mr Mahli's door as they walked past but he told them there was still no sign of Dylan. They felt quite despondent as they made their way through the streets, and didn't do their usual chattering about their latest Lego Technic invention or X Factor.

When they arrived at school it seemed that Mrs Best had also been infected by a bleak mood. Unusually she snapped at Danny when he told her he'd forgotten his PE kit and she didn't tell the children any funny stories about her weekend. The classroom was quiet and subdued all day and the children felt pretty glad to be going home at half past three.

'TB,' said Alys on the journey home, 'did you notice Mrs Best's eyes today?' TB shook his head. 'She looked mega-tired that's all. I've never seen bags like that on her before.'

'Maybe she'd had a tough weekend searching for a blooming irresponsible ghost or something!' replied TB.

'Aw, don't worry about Dylan; I'm sure he'll turn up soon. He's bound to be missing Mr Mahli. Or his cigars at least.' Alys smiled encouragingly at TB but he sniffed and looked away.

'Dylan was just about the coolest thing that's ever happened to me Al. We had a secret you know? We had this … this special job of looking after him and it was epic! When we knew we were going to be seeing Dylan in the shed or in Mrs Best's cupboard I felt … I dunno … like the colours were brighter or something.' TB blushed. 'It sounds stupid, but I really liked Dylan, and talking to him made me feel so excited, like I could do anything. I'm gutted he's gone Alys, I really am.'

Alys reached over and took hold of TB's hand. She completely understood because she felt just the same.

As the class cleared up ready for their lunchtime the next day, Mrs Best sat at the desk with one hand supporting her chin. She didn't ask for the best, most fabulous table. She didn't chivvy them along with promises of house points or magical prizes from the magical box of magical prizes. In fact she just looked downright miserable.

Gemma, who had been sitting at her desk, watching Mrs Best for a while, shot her hand up in the air.

'Yes Gemma?' asked Mrs Best.

'Are you OK, Mrs Best?' The class stopped tidying and fussing and turned to look at their teacher. She sat up straighter in her chair.

'What do you mean Gemma? Of course I'm OK.'

'It's just … you haven't been very happy so far this week and I've brought my homework in on time and

Danny's remembered the class rules all the time and so we don't know … you know, what's wrong with you.'

Mrs Best smiled fondly at Gemma. 'You are so sweet to notice that I've been a bit … well … rubbish. I hope I haven't been too much of a battle-axe.' The children waited for her to explain. Mrs Best sighed, stood up, walked round to the front of her desk and sat on it.

'Look,' she began, 'it's all very strange but something odd is happening to me and I just can't sleep with worry.' She looked as though she wasn't sure whether to tell the children but then took a deep breath and carried on.

'It all started last week. I went to bed one evening, in my tiger onesie of course, and I remembered I'd left the garden chair out. I always put it away at night so it doesn't get damp. So I got up (my husband was already snoring, he's a very heavy sleeper) to put it away. I went out the back door and picked up the chair to take to the shed at the bottom of my garden. It's quite big folded up so I couldn't really see where I was going. Anyway, I was right at the door of the shed when I tripped over something and fell on the grass, luckily on top of my chair. When I got up to look at what I'd tripped over I saw it was my lawnmower! Not only that but my plant pots and wheelbarrow and gardening tools were also on the floor around the shed!'

Mrs Best paused for a minute and looked at the children. They all stared back, anxious to hear the end of the story. Alys and TB were the only ones looking at each other instead of Mrs Best, looks of incredulity on their faces.

'So I went inside the shed,' Mrs Best continued 'although I was feeling a bit scared as you can imagine!'

'Was it a burglar, Miss?' shouted Gregory from the back of the class.

'No Gregory, nothing was missing. It had all just been moved. The weird thing was that the shed was completely empty. Nothing left in there at all, not even a spider's web on the ceiling!'

This was all beginning to sound frighteningly familiar to TB and Alys. Mrs Best went on to explain how she'd woken up her husband and they'd put everything back. She'd felt a little bit freaked out but managed to sleep anyway, thinking someone had just played a harmless trick on her.

The next day however, everything was out of the shed again. This time, as they started to put everything back, Mrs Best had heard a low moan and suddenly felt very cold. She'd rushed out of the shed in fright and hadn't felt able to go back in again since.

Mr Best had sorted out the shed only for the same thing to happen the next night. He tried waiting near the shed for the culprit to appear and had even fashioned a sort of trip wire around the garden perimeter (the children were quite impressed by this), but no one had come in and no one had gone out. It was all very peculiar and Mrs Best couldn't sleep at all, worrying about who was taunting her in this way.

'Have you ever heard anything like it?' Mrs Best asked the children with an anxious look on her pretty face. Alys and TB had. And they knew exactly what to do about it.

Sixteen

The Best Plan

'The crafty devil!' exclaimed Mr Mahli when the children told him what they knew after school. 'Whatever do you think he's doing in Mrs Best's shed then?'

'No idea,' replied TB, 'but we have to go and get him. Poor Mrs Best is freaking out!' Mr Mahli looked thoughtful for a minute.

'He must *want* her to know he's there,' he mused, 'or he wouldn't have made it so blooming obvious with all his furniture removal trickery. Wonder when he learnt that trick then. I don't know, travelling in bags, floating in cupboards; it sounds as though Dylan has been given a whole new lease of life with you two!'

'Why would he want her to know?' asked a worried Alys. 'Surely he doesn't want to scare her! What's she ever done to him? And why would he want to get *us* in trouble? We were epic to him! We were like, the best ever friends, taking him out and that.'

'Calm down lovely,' soothed Mr Mahli, 'I'm sure he doesn't want to get you into trouble. What you need to know about Dylan is that he's a little … impetuous.'

'What does that mean?' asked Alys.

'I know,' said TB, 'it means you don't give a monkeys about anyone else, just yourself. Dylan's off on his adventures and he hasn't given us a second thought.'

The children felt very cross with Dylan now and Mr Mahli went off to the kitchen to see if he had any of Nan Taylor's bara brith left. In times of distress, cake was always the answer.

'We need to go and get him,' repeated TB as he helped himself to a spoonful of mayonnaise (the cake was all gone unfortunately). 'We need to find out where Mrs

Best lives, go over without letting her know we're there and make him leave her shed.'

'You're right,' said Alys, 'but I can't go this evening 'cos I've got Tae Kwon-do.'

'And I'm … out between seven and eight thirty,' added Mr Mahli.

'Where are you off to?' Alys asked casually. She was surprised to see Mr Mahli was blushing! TB knew at once.

'Nan! You're going to see my Nan aren't you?' A big smirk spread across his face.

'She needed a bridge partner, Tomos. It's not a wedding son, calm down. Anyway, you can't go about stalking ghosts at night. Where does Mrs Best live? I'll go and get him myself.'

The children paused. They desperately wanted to be part of this mission but knew Mr Mahli would never let them. TB glanced at Alys and read her like a book. They'd go alright, but without Mr Mahli knowing about it.

'I'll google her Mr M,' he said and sat down at Mr Mahli's ancient PC.

He was still there thirty minutes later.

'Oh, TB! How are we supposed to find her house? You said you'd find it. What happened?' Alys demanded.

'I looked, alright? I googled her and checked her Facebook and Instagram and everything but I can't find her address. Don't panic though,' TB soothed, 'we'll just go to the school and look in the office. I know there's a file there with all the teachers' names and addresses and stuff and we can…'

'TB! You are not serious. We can't go breaking in to the school! Honestly, all these clandestine plans have gone to your head!' TB and Mr Mahli stared at Alys.

'Good Word!' they said in unison.

'It was "word of the day" last week.' Alys shrugged. 'Anyway, you're just going to have to leave it Mr M. Get him another night.' TB nodded reluctantly but Mr Mahli had disappeared into the hallway. When he came back he was holding a large floppy book.

'Here it is,' he announced, 'number 27, Sketty Avenue.' He looked up at the children with a smug

smile
on
his
face.

'Sometimes books beat computers you know,' he declared in quite an annoying voice.

TB and Alys left Mr Mahli to get ready, but they had no intention of letting him go alone.

'We'll have to follow him tonight Al,' TB announced as they crossed the road, 'under the cover of darkness.'

'Yes!' hissed Alys, punching the air; the balaclava was going to see some action after all.

The plan was set.

Seventeen

Operation 'Dylan'

TB pulled the covers right up to his chin when his mum came in to say goodnight, masking his black jumper and jeans. The moment his mum had turned off the light and gone back downstairs, TB jumped out of bed and headed to the window. He had climbed down several times from here before. It wasn't too bad because there was a little flat roof about three foot below the window and from there he could leap onto one of the garden tiers and run down the steps. But he'd never done it in the dark.

TB slipped his backpack over his shoulders, tucked his torch down his trousers and stepped out into the night. The air felt chilly around his face and he suddenly felt very alive. His breath came fast and shallow and the cool air in his lungs seemed to be pulsing around his whole body.

Alys waited until her parents had gone into the lounge, shut the door and put the telly on, then she sneaked straight out the front door. Despite the balaclava, she was less dramatic than TB as a rule.

They watched Mr Mahli leave the house from behind a handy rhododendron bush, then followed him, silently, as he hurried down the road.

Dark masters of the night.

Sketty Avenue was quiet and tree-lined. There were lampposts at regular intervals all along the street, but the one outside 27 was dark. TB vaguely wandered if Dylan had anything to do with that. He had a history of blowing bulbs after all.

The two friends stayed close to the brick wall as they shuffled round to the back of the house. A light was on in the front room downstairs, but the curtains were drawn so only a slice of yellow shone out onto the small front garden.

Alys reached for TB's hand in the dark. She was more scared of Mr Best lying in wait for them in the garden than she was of any spooks or ghouls. But she hoped it was too early for him to begin his nightly garden patrol. The back garden was eerily silent. The shed stood at the bottom of it, looking foreboding and slightly tilted. The pair stood very still for what seemed like a few minutes but was probably only one. When there was no sign of any other movement in the garden they forged ahead.

'Look out for Mr Best's trip wires,' warned Alys in a whisper. They began to walk differently then, with high steps like they were doing exaggerated

tip-toes. They looked quite ridiculous at that moment, but luckily no one was there to see them.

Except Mr Mahli.

He had cunningly camouflaged himself by holding a fern in front of his face and was creeping towards the shed a few steps in front of TB and Alys.

'Pssst!' TB hissed 'Mr M, it's us!' Mr Mahli jumped a metre in the air and threw his fern straight at TB. TB ducked to avoid the actually-not-very-scary plant and Alys put her finger to her lips.

'Shh. Mr Mahli. Calm down and keep quiet!' Mr Mahli frowned at this.

'Don't you go telling me what to do Miss Alys James. What the devil are you two doing here? Do your mums know you're here?'

The children looked shiftily at their feet for a moment.

'No,' started TB, 'but…'

'Don't make excuses boy. I told you not to come and you expressly disobeyed me. When I was your age I…'

'Mr Mahli,' whispered Alys, 'we've brought the bag.'

Mr Mahli stopped wagging his finger at the pair and looked at the rucksack TB was carrying on his back.

'The bag?'

'Yes' continued Alys 'how else can we get Dylan out of the shed?' Mr Mahli chewed his lip for a moment then quietly sighed.

'Come on then. But you're going straight home after this and there'll be no Joe's ice cream on the way.'

Alys reached the shed first. 'Right TB, look around for the key,' she instructed.

But this time the shed wasn't locked. The ease with which the door opened took TB by surprise and he stumbled backwards, letting the door bang against the side of the shed. 'Oh no!' whispered Alys and the three friends froze.

'Oh no!' exclaimed another voice in the darkness. It was a voice they knew well.

'Dylan boy!' called Mr Mahli, 'what are you up to eh? It's time to come home now. You've caused quite a bit of mischief.' TB shone the torch into the shed and there was Dylan, in another replica of Mr Mahli's shed, sitting comfortably in his old chair and holding a pen like a cigar between his lips.

TB, Mr Mahli and Alys piled into the shed and pulled the door shut behind them. 'We'll have to talk about it later,' urged TB. 'We've got to get you out of here before Mr or Mrs Best comes out and starts going mental.' But Dylan shook his head. 'Aw no! Don't do this to us, Dylan. You're scaring Mrs Best to pieces being here. She won't even come into her own shed any more. Why are you here Dylan? Why?'

Dylan lowered his pen-cigar and regarded TB. 'I'm here, boy,' he said slowly, 'because I'm in love with Mrs Best.' He paused to see their reactions then went on. 'And I'm going to tell her I'm here as soon as I find the opportunity. She and I will have wonderful times in this place together once she understands about me.'

The children were amazed. Mr Mahli sat down on the floor in shock. Nobody knew quite what to say. Could Dylan be serious? Did he really want to live here with Mrs Best? And did he really believe that she could love a ghost?

No one had the chance to answer these questions however, because there was a very loud knock on the shed door right at that moment.

Eighteen

A Shed Load of Trouble

They heard a nervous throat-clearing, then a shaky voice demanded loudly, 'Come out of that shed right now this instant. I've called the police and they're on their way.'

'Oh no,' groaned TB. 'You two stall him, I'll try to get Dylan in the bag.'

Mr Mahli and Alys stood side by side in the shed doorway, ready to block Mr Best's view, and opened the door. To say Mr Best was surprised to see an old man and a nine-year-old girl in his shed at half past nine on a Tuesday night would be an understatement.

'What are you … who are you … what? Who are you doing here?' babbled Mr Best, lowering the cricket bat he was carrying. Alys noticed Mrs Best

standing in a pool of light by the back door, her arms wrapped tightly around her middle.

'Mrs Best,' she called out suddenly, 'it's me, Alys.' Mr Best turned back towards his wife, who came running over the lawn towards them.

'Alys?' she cried. 'Has it been you all along? I don't understand…'

'No, Mrs Best, I wanted to help you. I was worried about what you said in school and I thought I could…'

'This is one of your pupils?' interrupted Mr Best.

'Yes,' Mrs Best confirmed, 'but I have no idea what she's doing here at this time of night and who this man is with her!' The couple turned to Mr Mahli, who opened his mouth to speak, then closed it abruptly when he realised he had nothing to say.

Alys came to his rescue. 'This is my granddad,' she said, desperately. 'He's great at doing this kind of thing you see because he worked as a commando in the war and had to do like, tons of stake-outs and stuff.' Mr Mahli smiled reassuringly at the couple. 'I asked him to come with us because I shouldn't be out at night without an adult of course, but I was so keen to help you get rid of the … whatever's been bothering you.'

Mrs Best sighed and smiled. 'You shouldn't have done this, Alys,' she said softly, 'but I really appreciate you trying to help. Look, come inside and warm up. We'll ring the police and tell them they don't need to come after all. Bring your … um … granddad too, come on.' Mrs Best ushered them all towards the house and Mr Mahli surreptitiously pushed the shed door shut behind them.

TB and Dylan narrowed their eyes at each other like cowboys preparing for a dual. 'I'm not coming with you boy, so you may as well leave,' Dylan declared. TB turned around without a word and stepped out of the shed. He was back a second later with two things in his hands: a box of screws and a hammer. He held them up for Dylan to see.

'Don't make me get nasty, Dylan,' he warned, 'but I know how to use this and I'm not afraid to do it.'

Dylan smirked lazily. 'You can't hurt me lad, I'm a ghost.' But TB just smirked right back at him.

'Oh, I'm not planning on hurting you, Spooky Simon.' (He didn't know where that came from, but thought it sounded good at the time.) 'I'm planning on fixing everything and anything I can possibly fix to the floor of this shed, and you won't be able to move it.'

Dylan opened his mouth to protest but TB went on, 'and when I've done that I'll start on the ceiling, and pretty soon you'll have no room to make your ghostly den and Mrs Best will never come in here anyway. Give it up, Dylan; you've got to come with me. It's not right you being here, you know that.'

Dylan stared first at the hammer in TB's hand and then back at the boy's face.

'Since when did nine year olds become so damn bossy?' he asked softly. He sank down further into his chair and put his messy-haired head in his hands.

'You can't understand yet boy, but she's cigars to me. She's the drinks I can't have and the silk I can't touch. Her voice is my heart's music and I can't go back to the quiet of Mr Mahli's shed, I just can't. I need beauty in my life boy, like you need water.'

TB smiled sadly and shrugged because it seemed like the right thing to do. He didn't have a clue what Dylan was on about but he had to get him out of the shed before Mr Mahli and Alys left the house and went home without him.

'Dylan, we'll find you some beauty I promise. But it can't be here. We really do have to go now … don't make me use the hammer.'

Nineteen

A Disgruntled Guest

The noises began a few days after Dylan's reluctant return to Mr Mahli's shed. He had been quite stubborn about visitors and the children had only been allowed in a couple of times to see him. It was Friday night when the banging sound became too loud for Mr Mahli to ignore. He poked his head out of the back door to see his shed rocking about in an alarming manner.

Dylan was running from side to side, bashing his body into the walls of the shed and ricocheting off to hit the other side again.

'For goodness sake Dylan, stop all this!' implored Mr Mahli. 'You'll wake up the neighbours! What are you trying to do anyway? Break the shed?'

Dylan stopped running about and sat on the floor in a heap.

'Actually yes, I was trying to break the shed. I'm fed up to the back teeth of this place, Mahli. I look out of the window every day and the view never changes. *My* view never changes. I miss Claire and I want to get out.'

'Claire?' Mr Mahli questioned.

'Mrs Best,' confirmed Dylan. 'My Claire, my light.'

'Good grief man, stop being so dramatic! Whoever heard of a ghost being in love? You're imagining it Dylan. You just need … I don't know … to forget about Mrs Claire. I'm off to bed now and I need you to leave my poor old shed alone. You've never managed to exist in the open air man, remember that.'

Mr Mahli left the shed, closing the door behind him. The noises had stopped but Mr Mahli felt just as troubled and he didn't know what to do.

On Saturday night Mr Mahli was woken up by Roy from number six knocking on his door.

'Whatever you're up to Mr Mahli, in that shed of yours, please can you leave it till the morning? We're all trying to get some sleep next door.' Mr Mahli apologised quickly and scuttled into the garden to tell Dylan off again.

He found Dylan sitting quietly in his seat. He was flickering gently round the edges and seemed quite transparent in the half-light.

'Dylan?' Mr Mahli asked gently. 'What's happening?'

Dylan glanced up but hardly seemed to see Mr Mahli. He closed his eyes and rocked slightly in his

116

chair. As Mr Mahli watched, his outline blurred and wobbled before becoming more solid again.

'Are you leaving us boy?' Mr Mahli crouched down next to Dylan and peered into his face.

'Just having a kip, Mahli, just having a kip,' he slurred and Mr Mahli crept quietly out of the shed and left him to sleep.

TB's mum called up the stairs on Sunday morning, 'Tomos, Mr Mahli's here for you!' and TB came sleepily down the stairs, rubbing his eyes.

'Hiya Mr M,' he yawned.

'Thanks Mrs Brown, I just need TB's help with something in the garden if he's free?' Mr Mahli smiled.

'Of course, no problem. Hey, my mum called by the way. She's ever so pleased with her new bridge partner,' she nudged Mr Mahli playfully. 'I'm sure she'd appreciate a call sometime.'

'Oh, lovely!' Mr Mahli blushed and looked suddenly awkward as TB's mum headed off into the kitchen humming to herself.

Mr Mahli turned to TB. 'Get dressed TB. We've got to do something about Dylan,' he said. And then he lowered his voice to a whisper. 'He's fading. I don't think we'll have him around much longer.'

TB didn't need to be told twice. He was dressed and in the shed before Mr Mahli had even returned from knocking on Alys' door. TB squinted in the dim light of the shed.

'You still here Dylan?' he called. His voice sounded much louder than necessary for the size of the shed. A thin murmur came back at him, and as TB's eyes adjusted to the light he saw a faint outline of a man, a desk and an old chair.

'Woah Dylan!' exclaimed TB. 'What's happening to you? I can hardly see you! And I was getting so pro at seeing you.'

He was surprised to hear the reply of a stronger voice: 'I'm still here lad. Just a bit tired, you know.' And surprisingly his outline seemed to strengthen a little.

Alys and Mr Mahli entered the shed at that moment and closed the door behind them. 'What is this?' asked a weak Dylan, 'the cavalry?' Mr Mahli laughed but Alys and TB just frowned.

'What can we do Dylan?' TB asked. 'How can we help you?'

'Take me out would you? Too many years in the same place … I have sores on my brain.'

Mr Mahli suddenly looked sad and Alys reached out to touch his arm.

'It's OK, Mr M,' she said. 'We'll take him, won't we TB? Hang on Dylan, we'll come for you tomorrow and take you back to school.' TB started to protest but a look from Alys silenced him.

'It's where he seemed the most alive,' she stated, and TB had to agree.

Twenty

A Welshman's Home is His Shed

Alys only remembered about the school trip when the children arrived at school the next day with Dylan in TB's backpack.

'Oh, pants!' she exclaimed, as she saw the bus spluttering beside the gates. 'Totally forgot we're off to the Space Centre today!'

TB groaned and pulled his backpack up to his lips.

'Don't worry Dylan,' he whispered, 'we'll set you up tidy in the cupboard and then…'

'No boy,' came a voice for the bag, 'take me with you.' The children looked at each other, unsure of what to do. Then Alys shrugged.

'It's by the sea,' she said. 'It might do him good.'

It wasn't until they were standing in the queue to enter the Space Centre that TB felt Dylan start to move. 'Keep still!' he urged through gritted teeth. But the backpack was jilting about pretty wildly now and TB had to jump about himself to hide it.

'Keep still, Tomos,' called Mrs Best as she went past counting heads. As the line of children began to move towards the entrance TB grabbed Alys' hand and pulled her out of the line behind a thick pillar. The rest of the class were chatting excitedly and didn't notice the two friends creep away from the Space Centre towards the wood at the edge of the car park.

'Woah TB! We're going to get in mahooosive trouble!' exclaimed Alys with a huge grin on her face.

'Yeah I know,' replied TB, 'but I couldn't go in there with Dylan jumping about.' As he heard his name, Dylan pushed at the drawstring and poked his ghostly head out of the bag.

'That's better!' he said. 'Where are we going then?'

The children traipsed through the dank wood next to the centre, enjoying the smells and the quiet and the feeling that they were great explorers, as Dylan chatted merrily in the bag. He seemed so much better out of the shed that Alys and TB started to wonder if he wasn't putting it on all along, just to get them to take him back to Mrs Best. But it wasn't being close to Mrs Best that had cheered Dylan up this time. He was outside, he was somewhere new, he could smell the ocean.

 'Wow! Check this out!' called Alys as she rounded a large oak tree. TB followed behind her and saw that they'd emerged out of the other side of the wood, on to a cliff. The sea stretched out below them and sea birds swooped and laughed in the wind. The air smelt beautifully fresh and the friends stood in silence for a minute just breathing it in.

'What do you think, Dylan?' asked TB, holding the backpack up in front of him. But Dylan didn't reply. He stared wistfully at the open view in front of him. TB noticed his eyes were glassy and when he blinked, a tiny bit of moisture seemed to stick on his eyelashes.

Alys had been looking around.

'You have to come and see this, TB and Dylan, you are so gonna love this!' She led them back the way she had come, tripping and stumbling over roots and branches in her hurry. After a minute she suddenly stopped.

'Ta-dah!' she cried, stretching her arms in the air. TB looked around.

'What Al? What you on about?'

'I found it!' she replied, 'it's just the perfect place for Dylan!' Alys turned and began to tug at the branches behind her. It was then that TB saw that the leaves were covering a wooden structure with a moss-covered corrugated iron roof.

'I squeezed around the front to get a better look,' Alys said breathlessly, 'and there's a window that looks out to the sea! No one's been in here for years, it's perfect, so secret!'

As Dylan watched from the bag on the floor, Alys and TB pulled at the ivy that was covering the door and prised at the wood with their fingers.

'We are such shed-breaking experts now, Al,' stated TB as the door swung open. Inside the shed was full of weeds and old pots. A couple of cardboard boxes had rotted away and their contents spilled messily onto the floor.

Dylan smiled. 'Get me in then. We'll have this shipshape in no time.'

After an hour of hard work Alys and TB stood back and looked at the shed. Dylan had already begun his magic and they could see the outlines of his desk, chair and bookcase slowly materialising. Dylan himself was becoming more solid by the minute.

'This is it, kids. This is it.' He rubbed his palms together as he stared out of his new window at the glistening sea and the darkening clouds.

The children stared at his round face, lit up like a child's on Christmas morning and smiled. TB nudged Alys. 'Look!' he nodded towards Dylan's hand. A pen was appearing between his fingers and a little leather-bound book became visible on the desk, next to his other hand.

'Dylan, are you going to write something?' Alys asked, quickly startling Dylan out of his far-away thoughts. He looked down in surprise at the pen in his hand.

'Well, yes. It looks like I am!' and his accompanying chuckle was so loud and so rich that the children couldn't help joining in. He turned to look at them then. 'I remember now kids. It's the stories and the words that I need and here, in this wild, golden place, they're coming back to me. I can feel them bubbling up in here,' he thumped his fist on his belly. 'You can leave me here happy, Prince Tomo and Princess Alys, I know what I have to do now.'

Suddenly Dylan laughed, as a longhaired ginger cat pushed her way in through the door at that moment. He held out his arms almost as though he were expecting her.

The cat purred and wound her way around Dylan's legs. He sighed and nodded at the children.

'You see, I won't be lonely. I have this cat and the sea is always changing, and children will visit the beach down there in summer too. I'm going to be fine.

'You two had better get going. Mrs Best doesn't deserve all the worry,' he added softly.

Alys and TB picked up their bags from the floor.

'Bye then, Dylan. I think you'll be happy here,' Alys smiled. TB just held up a hand in a silent salute and turned to go.

Just as they opened the door, Dylan called out, 'TB, Tomos lad, come here. You too, Alys,' and the children ran back towards the shimmering man as fast as they could. He held out his not-arms and TB and Alys fell into them. The strangest sensation overcame the children at that moment; they suddenly felt a warmth coming from Dylan, and his arms felt briefly solid. Then, as quickly as it had come, the feeling disappeared and Alys and TB let go of their ghostly friend and backed towards the door.

'Say so long to Mr Mahli for me won't you?' asked Dylan.

'Course. We'll tell him where to find you, he can come and visit,' said TB shakily.

'Tell him thanks for everything, OK?' The children nodded, then they left before they could start to cry and were running back through the trees so quickly they didn't hear the sob of a grown man in the woods behind them, or the gentle meow of a cat.

Twenty-one

Mr Mahli's Shed

Mr Mahli listened quietly to the children's story that evening. He couldn't believe no one had noticed they were missing from the Space Centre, and thought it was a real stroke of luck that Mrs Best had let the class have a little play in the woods before they got back on the bus, so TB and Alys had managed to re-join them without anyone noticing.

He looked a little sad when they told him about Dylan's new home, but smiled at them kindly and told them they had done the right thing. Alys tried to describe the look of happiness on Dylan's face, his joy at the idea of writing by the sea and his delight when the ginger cat turned up, and Mr Mahli had cleared his throat squeakily and said he understood. And he *had* understood, because happiness is everything, and Dylan was his friend.

The days after that became cooler as the winter began to settle in to Swansea. TB and Alys found themselves visiting Mr Mahli's garden less and less as the nights came in earlier and rain arrived like an unwanted visitor almost daily.

One night Alys' parents were going down The Chattery to see a band and asked if Alys could stay over at TB's house. Alys had settled down in the spare room but was woken up in the middle of the night by a very strange noise. Spooked, she ran into TB's room and shook him awake.

'TB! Wake up you muppet, can't you hear that noise?' she whispered loudly. TB jerked awake and sat bolt upright in bed.

'Al? You scared me to death! What are you doing?'

'Come and look at this,' said Alys, her voice strangely far away in the darkness. TB climbed out of bed and padded across the landing to the spare room at the front of the house.

The light was coming from the back of Mr Mahli's house. And it wasn't just green. Purple and orange lights sparkled and shimmered against the dark sky. The noise Alys had heard was getting slightly louder now; it was a sort of whirring and humming and seemed to be coming from the same place as the lights.

'What's Mr Mahli up to this time?' TB mused. 'Come on Alys, let's check it out.'

They wrapped up in dressing gowns and slippers and crept past TB's parents' room like the ninjas they were.

As they crossed the street the sound got louder and the lights became brighter. Alys and TB didn't bother knocking on the front door but slipped around the side of the house to the back garden. TB was in front and stopped abruptly as he reached the garden so Alys bashed straight into his back.

'Oof! Thanks, TB,' she moaned. 'Could've warned me!' But then she stopped and looked over at Mr Mahli's shed; a look of sheer amazement on her face.

The shed was glowing with all sorts of coloured lights, but the brightest of these was coming from the bottom, which was hovering about a foot off the ground. The whirring sound seemed to be coming from a propeller that the children could see underneath the shed and something was popping and causing little puffs of smoke to surround it. Peering closely, the children could see Mr Mahli in the shed window. Just as he spotted them and started to wave, the strangest thing of all happened: the shed began to rise. Slowly at first, it wobbled and hesitated before gaining a surge of power and bolting straight up into the night sky. Mr Mahli waved down at the children who slowly lifted their hands and waved back at him.

It was so quiet after the shed finally disappeared above the clouds. The garden seemed eerily empty and the children realised they'd been holding their breath and suddenly shivered with the cold. Alys and TB didn't say a word as they turned to TB's house and headed back to bed, but their dreams that night were full of Mr Mahli's stories; of pirates and time travel; of ghosts and fireworks. And where other people would just see sheds, they knew they would always see magic.

Epilogue

Four weeks went by before the children saw Mr Mahli again. They had looked out for him and whizzed around the back of his house several times looking for the shed. But the house was still and the garden quiet and Mr Mahli seemed well and truly gone.

It was a cold but sunny Saturday when TB's nan popped round.

'Hiya Tom bach, I'm just dropping off this cake for you then I'm heading over … um…'

She wandered into the kitchen with a large tin-foiled cake and returned a second later re-wrapping the cake, which was now half the size. TB frowned.

'Nan, you've either got the biggest appetite in South Wales today or you're taking half my cake somewhere else.'

'It's not *your* cake Tomos Brown. And this bit's for your old friend Mr Mahli so stop complaining,' Nan retorted.

'Oh, but he's gone,' TB said. 'We haven't seen him for weeks. Didn't Mum say? We think he might have gone back to … India.' TB expected Nan to pull a sad expression but she laughed.

'TB, he's home! He sent me an Instagram picture. Look.' She proudly held up her phone for TB to see a picture of a table with a wooden board with little circles on it.

'What's that?' TB asked.

'Backgammon,' Nan replied. 'It's a game. He's invited me over for a game so I'm taking the cake and I'm going over. Is that OK?' Nan didn't wait for a reply. She shouted a 'Cheerio' to TB's mum, ruffled TB's hair and started for the door. TB stood, frozen to the spot for a second, then spurted out of the house after Nan. They were astonished to see Mr Mahli open up his front door to her with a cheery smile and invite her in!

TB was desperate to confront Mr Mahli and ask him a ton of questions but he couldn't in front of Nan so he darted round to Alys' house instead and the pair of them crept around the back to look at the shed.

It was strange to see it sitting there so innocently. There was no sign of Dylan and no sign of lights or smoke. It was just a shed.

TB helped Alys up onto his shoulders so she could look in through the smeary window but she reported down that it was still empty. Everything looked just the same except…

'Hang on,' Alys whispered 'don't put me down yet. What's that?'

TB didn't know. He couldn't see. But it sounded to him – and it sounds to me – like the start of a new adventure.

What do you think?

Here are some lines from 'Fernhill', a poem by Dylan Thomas.

Now as I was young and easy under the apple boughs

About the lilting house and happy as the grass was green,

The night above the dingle starry,

Time let me hail and climb

Golden in the heydays of his eyes,

And honoured among wagons I was prince of the apple towns

And once below a time I lordly had the trees and leaves

Trail with daisies and barley

Down the rivers of the windfall light.

Cut out the words, if you like, and see if you can move them around to make your own poem.